Licensed exclusively to Top That Publishing Ltd
Tide Mill Way, Woodbridge, Suffolk, IP12 1AP, UK
www.topthatpublishing.com
Text copyright © 2014 Trudi Granger
Illustrations copyright © 2014 Tide Mill Media
All rights reserved
0 2 4 6 8 9 7 5 3 1
Printed and bound in China

Illustrated by Gareth Llewhellin
Written by Trudi Granger

ISBN 978-1-78244-475-6

A catalogue record for this book is available from the British Library

Always There Bear

by Trudi Granger

'To my nearest and dearest, with love.'

Everyone needs a bear that's always there ...

A sunny, sandy seaside bear.

A much too wet to go outside bear.

A play-day with a friend at home bear.

A read a book alone bear.

A very happy birthday bear.

A sulky, grouchy, grumpy bear.

An in the car ... or bus
... or train bear.

A scoot ... or ride a trike ... or bike bear.

A full of bounce from toes to head bear.

A sore throat and snuffly nose in bed bear.

A splashing, sploshing in a puddle bear.

A very quiet, need a cuddle bear.

A playing together in the park bear.

A stay close, keep safe after dark bear.

An icy, snowy, all gone white bear.

A bright and blowy, fly a kite bear.

Everyone needs a bear that's always there ...

...An all day ... all night ... goodnight bear.